To Three Special Sisters—
Rose, Kay, and Fran
　　—Harriet Lerner and Susan Goldhor

To Rachel and Lily—
　　—Catharine O'Neill

What's So Terrible About Swallowing an Apple Seed?

By Harriet Lerner and Susan Goldhor

Illustrated by Catharine O'Neill

HARPERCOLLINSPUBLISHERS

One day, Rosie and her big sister, Katie, were sitting in their favorite tree eating crisp red apples.

"*Crunch, crunch, crunch,*" crunched Rosie.

"*Munch, munch, munch,*" munched Katie.

Crunching and munching and munching and crunching, Rosie and Katie ate their apples right down to the core.

Suddenly Rosie said, "I swallowed an apple seed! Whoops! I swallowed another one," and she giggled.

"Oh, no," said Katie in her most worried voice. "Watch out!"

"Why?" asked Rosie. "What's so terrible about swallowing an apple seed?"

Katie thought fast. "Well," she said, trying to sound smart, "that apple seed is going to grow into a tree right inside your stomach. That's what's so terrible."

"But how can it grow into a tree inside my stomach?" asked Rosie.

"It's easy," answered Katie. "It's nice and warm down there. It's just the right place for a seed to grow."

Rosie thought for a long time. "But trees need sunshine to grow. It's dark in my stomach."

"Well, of course," said Katie. Like most big sisters, she always had an answer for everything. "It's dark in the ground, too, when you plant seeds there. But when the branches of your apple tree get big enough, they'll grow out of your ears and get all the sunshine they need."

Rosie sat very still. She thought she could feel the tree starting to grow inside her stomach.

"What should I do, Katie?" she asked.

"Let's keep it secret till the branches start to show," said Katie.

"Okay," said Rosie. She always thought that her big sister knew best.

Every night Rosie asked Katie to look in her ears with a flashlight to see how the apple tree was growing.

Every night Katie said, "I can see it! I can see it! I'm almost sure I can see the tip of a branch down there!"

And every night Rosie could not fall asleep for a long time. She could feel her ears itching, and she tried to imagine what she would look like with apple tree branches growing out of her ears. Rosie imagined a lot of problems.

None of her hats would fit.

She wouldn't fit through the school-bus door.

No more somersaults and handstands!

Or jump rope!

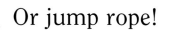

Good-bye, haircuts!
She would have to go
to the woodcutter instead.

All she could be when she grew up
was a coat rack.

Rosie felt very sad.

Pretty soon Katie began to feel sad, too.

She knew a seed couldn't really grow in Rosie's stomach. And she hadn't known that a lie could grow so big, just like a seed grows into a tree. The bigger the lie got, the harder it was for Katie to tell Rosie the truth. So she used her imagination to cheer Rosie up. Every night she would sit on Rosie's bed and tell her all the good things about having branches growing out of her ears.

Rosie could reach up and pick an apple
any time she wanted.

When they went to the beach, they would always
have a shady spot to sit.

If Rosie got lost at the ball game,

they would always be able to find her.

Rosie would never get lost again.

All their friends could climb up
and play on the branches.

On birthdays they could decorate her
branches with ribbons and candles.

All the animals would be her friends.

Rosie felt much better. She told her friend Bonnie that she had a special secret.

"Tell me! Tell me!" begged Bonnie. "I'm your best friend."

Rosie handed Bonnie the flashlight. "Look in my ears," she said.

"I don't see anything," Bonnie said. "Just a little ear dirt."

"Don't you see a branch?" asked Rosie.

"Nope," said Bonnie.

Rosie thought about this for a long time. She got madder and madder. Then she went and found Katie.

"Bonnie looked in my ear," she told her big sister, "and she didn't see any tree! You told me a lie!"

Katie said, "I can't help it if you believe everything I say!" But inside she was glad that the lie was finally over. She hugged Rosie and said she was sorry.

"It's okay," Rosie said. "But I was starting to like my apple tree."

The itch in Rosie's ears went away, and that night when she got into bed she thought how nice it was to be like everybody else. But as she was falling asleep, she started to feel a little bit sad.

"Katie," Rosie said, "I miss my apple tree!"

Katie understood. So she told Rosie a wonderful
story about a little girl with apple tree branches
growing out of her ears. In the spring, the little
girl's head would be covered with apple
blossoms. In the summer, birds would build
nests and squirrels would play in her branches.
In the fall, she would bring apples
to school for everyone
to eat.

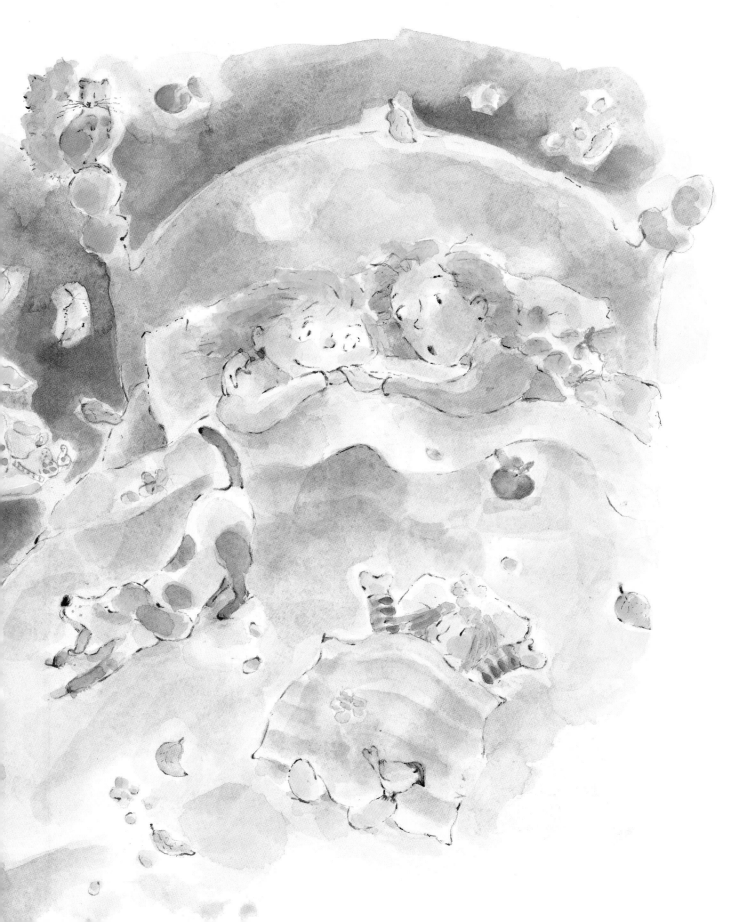

And before Katie even got to winter,

Rosie was fast asleep.

What's So Terrible About Swallowing an Apple Seed? Text
copyright © 1996 by Harriet Goldhor Lerner and Susan
Goldhor Illustrations copyright © 1996 by Catharine O'Neill
Printed in the U.S.A. All rights reserved. Library of Congress
Cataloging-in-Publication Data Lerner, Harriet. What's so
terrible about swallowing an apple seed? / by Harriet Lerner and
Susan Goldhor ; illustrated by Catharine O'Neill. p.   cm.
Summary: When Rosie swallows an apple seed, her sister
Katie tells her that an apple tree will grow out of her ears.
ISBN 0-06-024523-9. — ISBN 0-06-024524-7 (lib. bdg.)
[1. Sisters—Fiction. 2. Honesty—Fiction.] I. Goldhor, Susan.
II. O'Neill,   Catharine, ill. III. Title. PZ7.L5595Wh 1996
94-2769 [E]—dc20 CIP AC Typography by Al Cetta
1 2 3 4 5 6 7 8 9 10 ❖   First Edition